Books may be purchased in quantity and/or special sales by contacting the publisher, Build-a-Bow LLC , by email at Buildabowllc@gmail.com

Published by: Build-a-Bow , LLC, Racine, Wisconsin
Interior Design by: Karee Upendo
Cover Design by: Karee Upendo, Karee Couture
First Edition
Printed in U.S.A

I dedicate this book to my baby brother, Aven. Remember to always be yourself, everyone comes into the world with a special gift and purpose. Stay true to who you are, and never let anyone take your joy. Remember to be kind always, and treat others how you want to be treated. Love is the universal language of the world. Thank you to my mom Karee & dad Avery for teaching me, to love & treat everyone equally.

Xoxo - Alex

Bullies, bowties and brilliant Alex

By: Alex Hart-Upendo

Published by: Build-A-Bow LLC

Printed in the U.S.A

THIS IS ALEX, A BOY WHO LOVES TO LEARN HE GETS GOOD GRADES IN RETURN.

HE LEARNED AND LEARNED AND LEARNED AND LEARNED
BUT, ALEX'S TEACHER WAS CONCERNED.

SHE WAS WORRIED, ALEX WAS LEARNING TOO FAST. THE OTHER KIDS, HAD NOT EVEN FINISHED THEIR TASKS.

SHE GAVE HIM A TEST AND SURE TO SEE – ALEX TESTED
GIFTED, HE WAS AS BRIGHT AS CAN BE!

HIS CLASS DID NOT UNDERSTAND WHY HE WAS SO FAST, THEY WERE UPSET THAT THEY FINISHED LAST.

THEY CALLED HIM NAMES BECAUSE HE WAS SMART.
SOME EVEN SAID "ALEX, THE SMART TART."

NOBODY WANTED TO BE ALEX'S FRIEND, THEY
WOULDN'T EVEN LET HIM PLAY PRETEND.

ALEX WAS SAD HE HAD NO FRIENDS, HE ATE LUNCH ALONE
FOR DAYS ON END.

ALEX'S MOM SEEN HE WAS SAD, SHE WANTED TO
CHEER HIM UP AND MAKE HIM LAUGH.

HIS MOM IS A FASHION DESIGNER, SHE MAKES LOTS OF CLOTHES. ROWS AND ROWS AND ROWS OF CLOTHES!

SHE DECIDED TO TAKE ALEX TO A FASHION SHOW. HE REPLIED, "IF YOU SAY SO."

AT THE SHOW ALEX CHEERED UP, HE SEEN SO MANY
CLOTHES AND PEOPLE DOLLED UP.

ALEX WANTED TO BE LIKE HIS MOM, HE SAID "MAKING CLOTHES WOULD BE THE BOMB! "

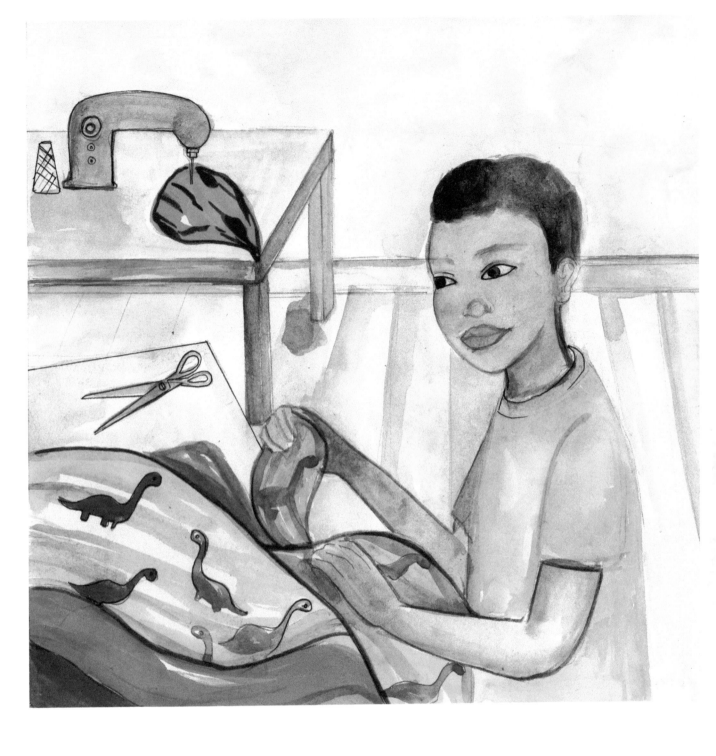

HE STARTED WITH FABRICS AND COLORS GALORE, HE
EVEN HAD SOME WITH DINOSAURS.

HIS MOM TAUGHT HIM HOW TO MAKE SOMETHING
EASY, A SIMPLE BOW-TIE WAS EASY PEACHY!

HE WORE IT TO SCHOOL AND HE WAS SO HAPPY, THE
OTHER KIDS EVEN SAID HE LOOKED SNAZZY.

NOW EVERYONE WANTED TO BUY A BOW, SO HE
STARTED A BUSINESS CALLED BUILD-A-BOW.

BOW AFTER BOW AFTER BOW AFTER BOW, HIS INNER
HAPPINESS STARTED TO SHOW!

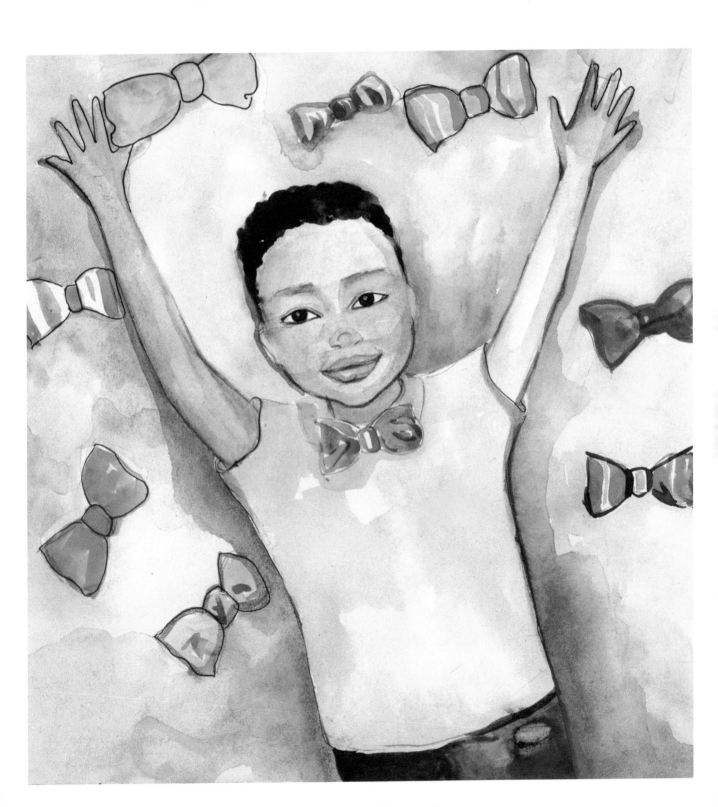

HE NEVER AGAIN ATE LUNCH ALONE, AND THE OTHER
KIDS SAID SORRY FOR LEAVING HIM ALONE.

ALEX TAUGHT EVERYONE THAT IT'S OKAY, TO BE YOURSELF IN DIFFERENT WAYS.

NO TWO PEOPLE ARE THE SAME, EVEN IF YOU SHARE THE SAME NAME.

REMEMBER TO TREAT OTHERS HOW YOU WANT TO BE TREATED, NOBODY DESERVES TO BE MISTREATED.

AUTHOR BIO:

At 10 years old, the Racine, WI resident has got a keen sense for fashion & business. Since the age of 5, the now fourth-grader has been building the foundation of his own budding fashion and special events business.

Aptly titled Build a Bow LLC, the company started out as custom bow-tie retailer, but has grown to include special events, where Alex provides attendees with the materials and instruction they need to make their very own bow ties & hair bows.In addition to offering event goers with choices of colorful and zany fabrics for designing hair bows or bow ties, he also lets them draw on their own piece of blank canvas, so they make a bow from a print uniquely their own. The company started when Alex at the age of 5 tested as gifted, his IQ was higher than most children in his age group. His gift was the staple of being isolated & bullied. He wanted to take the term nerd & turn it into something cool. Build-a-Bow LLC was created from being bullied to bow ties. That's what truly make Build-a-Bow unique, the founder & CEO is 10 years old.

Alex, lost his grandfather, famed University of Wisconsin-Madison football player Eddie "The Pony" Hart to cancer, he wants to become a biochemist so that he can find a cure for the disease. The loss of his grandfather is what inspired him to expand Build-a-Bow into a non profit community project. Forty percent of proceeds go back into the community. Build-a-Bow hosts a community workshop once a month, free of charge to all Racine patrons. At the workshop patrons are taught how to design a bow-tie. Each workshops bow-tie designs, are then sent off to awareness groups. For example September's awareness is Childhood cancer, the bow-ties designed at that month's workshop will go to children battling cancer.

 His community project was recognized by the state of Wisconsin, & Governor Scott Walker. Alex received a Proclamation, & his very own day (September,30th) for the philanthropy he has done in Racine, WI. Alex was the 2016 nominee award winner of the Apollo business award, presented by RMAC of Racine. He won the 2017 Humanitarian award, for Racine, he was even noticed by NBC & made a guest appearance on the day time television series, The Harry Connick Jr. Show.

Alex hopes to expand his company outside of Racine & continue to touch the lives of many one bow-tie a time. One of his biggest challenges is coincidentally the same thing that makes him unique, his age. Alex is the CEO & president of Build-a-Bow LLC so being available for his company needs & balancing school is tough. He has great dreams of being a Bio-Chemist so academic success is very important as well.

He hopes to one day have a community center & give people a place to create art free of charge. Philanthropy through art is one of the CEO passions.

CPSIA information can be obtained
at www.ICGtesting.com
Printed in the USA
LVHW072010250119
605319LV00002B/5/P